A DAY IN THE LIFE OF
T. REX

RED SHED

Contents

Introduction

Millions of years before the world had seen a human, the ground trembled under the feet of dinosaurs.

Let's travel back in time to discover more about one of the fiercest dinosaurs that ever lived.

Meet T. rex

Tyrannosaurus rex (or T. rex for short) is the most famous dinosaur ever to walk the Earth. T. rex was huge, heavy and horribly fierce.

Tyrannosaurus rex means 'tyrant lizard king'.

T. rex was nearly three times taller than a human being.

Terrifying teeth

When T. rex was hungry, other creatures lived in fear. T. rex had razor-sharp teeth and one bite from its gigantic jaws could crush their bones to crumbs!

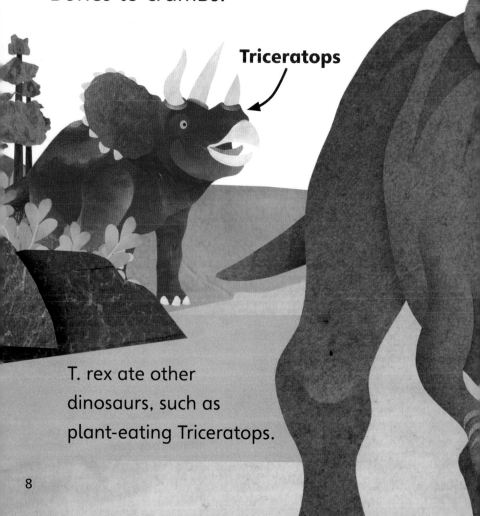

Triceratops

T. rex ate other dinosaurs, such as plant-eating Triceratops.

T. rex ripped through so much flesh that it grew a new set of teeth every few years.

T. rex could eat the weight of a lion in a single gulp.

Hunting for food

Having terrifying teeth didn't always mean an easy dinner. The forests were thick with trees and flowers, but these were not at all tasty to T. rex.

Mammals, such as Alphadon, would hide in burrows or branches.

Alphadon

Dinosaurs were **reptiles**, just like lizards.

Plenty of **insects** buzzed around, but they didn't make a good meal for T. rex.

bee

dragonfly

Tracking down treats

Luckily T. rex had good eyesight and a strong sense of smell. These were perfect for detecting other dinosaurs. T. rex could sniff out trails of freshly laid dung or even a rotting dead body.

Quetzalcoatlus

Quetzalcoatlus was the biggest flying animal ever. From tip to tip its wings were II metres!

Dead animals were easy meat for T. rex. Although sometimes pesky **pterosaurs**, such as Quetzalcoatlus, could swoop in first.

Struthiomimus

Chasing Struthiomimus

Some food needed chasing. T. rex ran
on two powerful back legs. It stuck out
its neck to balance the massive weight
of its head.

Struthiomimus means 'ostrich mimic'.

At full sprint, Struthiomimus was over twice as fast as T. rex!

Dinosaur race

A charging T. rex could move fast for its size. But it wasn't as fast as some of its nippy neighbours or the world's fastest human.

The fastest human can reach speeds of about 44 kilometres per hour.

T. rex

Its top speed was about 30 kilometres per hour.

Struthiomimus

Its top speed was about 80 kilometres per hour.

Ornithomimus

Its top speed was about 64 kilometres per hour.

Even super-tough T. rex felt
feeble against a thrashing
Ankylosaurus tail.

Ankylosaurus battle

Running around was tiring, and T. rex needed energy to roar. It could easily catch up with Ankylosaurus, but T. rex had to watch out for its bony armour and tail.

Ankylosaurus

Under the sea

Resting by the swooshing sea, T. rex could watch birds fishing. There were lots of tasty things to eat in the oceans but T. rex wasn't a great swimmer. Imagine trying to doggy paddle with those arms!

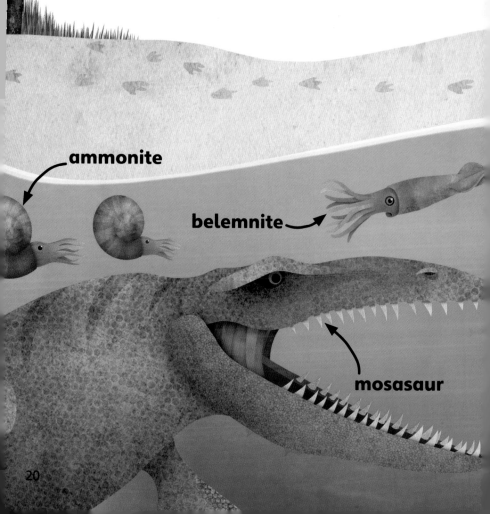

ammonite

belemnite

mosasaur

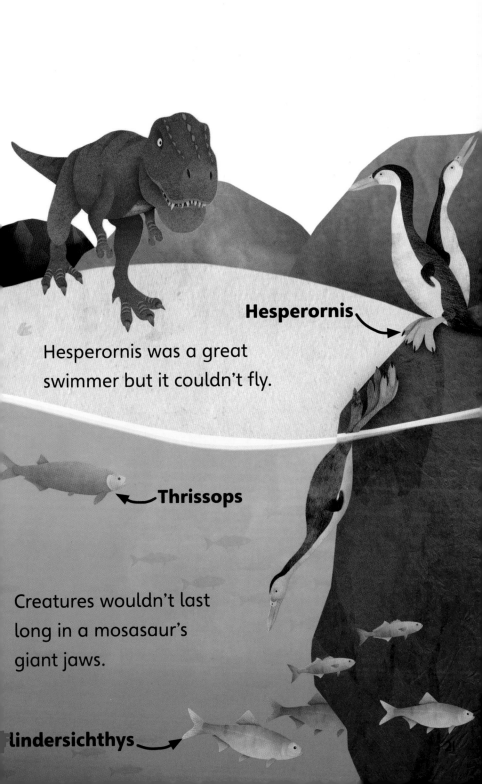

Hesperornis

Hesperornis was a great swimmer but it couldn't fly.

Thrissops

Creatures wouldn't last long in a mosasaur's giant jaws.

lindersichthys

Edmontosaurus herd

Edmontosaurus herds could be found chomping on twigs in a swamp. Their cheek teeth were perfect for mashing up chewy plants. However, their duck-like bill was no good for fighting.

←— **Edmontosaurus**

Edmontosaurus had about 1,000 teeth hidden in its cheeks but none in its beak.

A feast of one Edmontosaurus could keep T. rex going for a week. There might even be some meat spare for the rest of the family!

All baby dinosaurs hatched from eggs.

The end of T. rex

One day a huge space rock crashed into Earth and threw up dust clouds that blocked out the sun. The world became dark and cold for a very long time. This caused the dinosaurs to eventually die out.

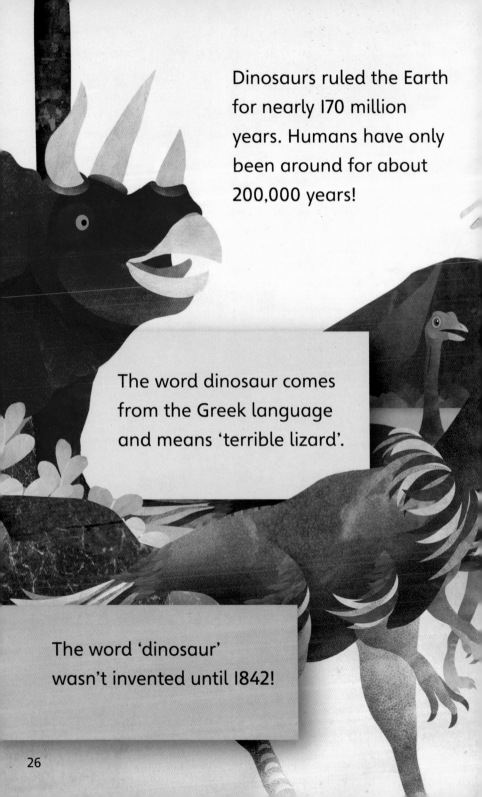

Dinosaurs ruled the Earth for nearly 170 million years. Humans have only been around for about 200,000 years!

The word dinosaur comes from the Greek language and means 'terrible lizard'.

The word 'dinosaur' wasn't invented until 1842!

The most complete T. rex **skeleton** was found in South Dakota, USA. It was nicknamed Sue.

The first dinosaur to be named was Megalosaurus ('great lizard') in 1824.

Dinosaur facts

So far we've found and named more than 00 types of dinosaur.

Age of the dinosaurs

The first dinosaurs appeared around 252 million years ago. T. rex lived about 68–66 million years ago. This was during the Cretaceous Period.

Triassic Period
252–201 million years ago

Jurassic Period
201–145 million years ago

Cretaceous Period
145–66 million years ago

How do we know dinosaurs existed?

Skeletons are one way we know about dinosaurs today. Over millions of years they've hardened into rocks called **fossils**. Here are some of the other fossils that have been found.

dinosaur egg

The largest fossil of a dinosaur egg was laid by Hypselosaurus. It was the size of 73 chicken eggs.

chicken egg

The biggest dinosaur poo fossil to be discovered was 64cm long. It was full of crushed bones and probably came from a T. rex.

Pronunciation guide

Alphadon	AL-fa-don
Ankylosaurus	an-KIE-loh-SORE-us
Edmontosaurus	ed-MON-toe-SORE-us
Flindersichthys	FLIN-derz-IK-theez
Hesperornis	HESS-per-OR-niss
Hypselosaurus	hip-SELL-oh-SORE-us
Megalosaurus	MEG-a-lo-SORE-us
Mosasaur	moh-zuh-SORE
Ornithomimus	orn-ITH-oh-MEE-mus
Pterosaur	TEH-ro-SORE
Quetzalcoatlus	KWET-zal-koh-AT-lus
Struthiomimus	STRUTH-ee-oh-MEE-mus
Triceratops	trie-SERRA-tops
Tyrannosaurus rex	tie-RAN-oh-SORE-us rex

Glossary

fossils   Parts of an animal that have turned into rock.

insects   Small creatures with six legs and a body formed of three parts, such as bees or ants.

mammals   Warm-blooded animals, such as dogs or humans.

pterosaurs   Flying reptiles that lived alongside the dinosaurs.

reptiles   Cold-blooded animals that lay eggs and are covered in scales, such as lizards or dinosaurs.

skeleton   The framework of bones that supports the body of an animal or a human.

Index